GUMDROP

A British Motorcar (Vintage)
Austin Clifton Heavy 12/4, 5 seater tourer
Made in 1926
Owner: Mr Josiah Oldcastle

BUNBO

An Asian Elephant (Elephas maximus)
Proboscidean mammal of the family Elephantidae
Born in 1970
Owner: Mr Barmy Bigshott

For Mimi, with my love.

GUMDROP
and the Elephant

Written and illustrated by
Val Biro

AWARD PUBLICATIONS LIMITED

One day Mr Josiah Oldcastle went for a drive in Gumdrop, his trusty old car. Round a bend he saw a battered gate with a sign over it. It said:

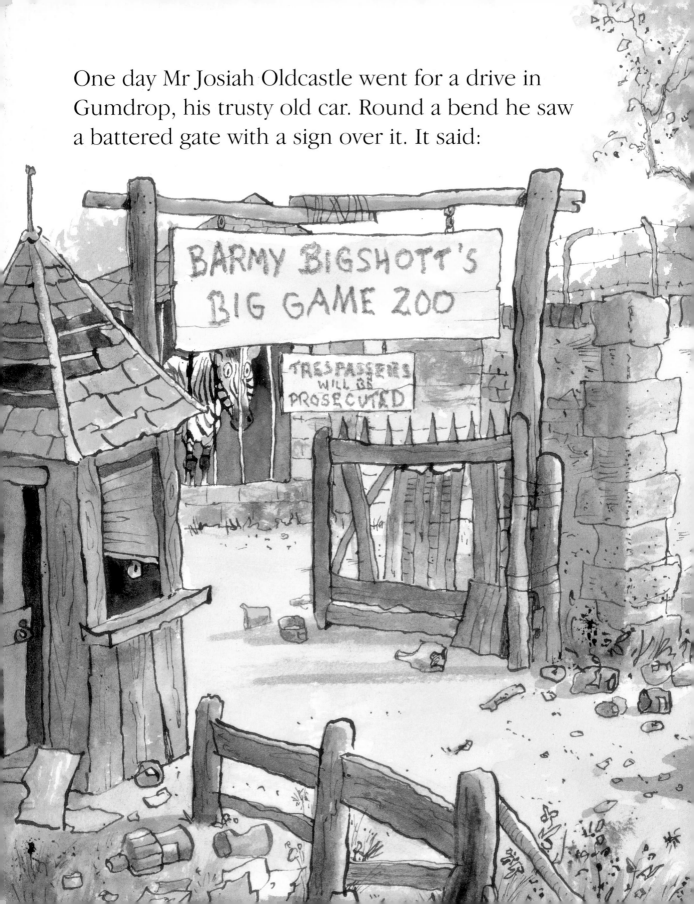

"Let's go in, Grandad," cried Dan from the back, "I'd love to see the animals." Mr Oldcastle liked animals too, only this zoo looked so run-down. But as Dan insisted, Mr Oldcastle agreed and drove in.

Inside it was even worse. The animals looked hungry and miserable in their cramped cages. Hungriest of all was Bunbo the elephant, so Dan gave him a bun.

"Stop feedin' them beasts!" roared a man with a gun. It was Barmy Bigshott. "Get out, we're closed!" He was so nasty that Horace the dog snarled and leaped at him.

"And take this dog and that scrap'eap of a car with you!" bellowed Bigshott.

Mr Oldcastle was furious. Scrapheap indeed! So back he shouted, "This zoo is a total disgrace and I'll report you for cruelty to animals!"

And as he drove Gumdrop out, Bigshott bawled, "Report? I'll give you report!" and he fired his gun with a thunderous BANG!

"That Bigshott's really barmy," growled Mr Oldcastle as he drove outside the crumbling wall. There was a big gap in it, and suddenly an elephant stepped straight through! When he saw Gumdrop he looked alarmed and galumphed away.

"It's Bunbo!" cried Dan, "he must have escaped. Let's go after him!" But Gumdrop's engine had stalled and there was no way to get him back.

"Except with this," said Mr Oldcastle
as he honked the horn in a way that made
it sound like an elephant trumpeting.
Bunbo stopped and trumpeted back,
sounding just like Gumdrop.

He must have thought that the car
was another elephant, so he came
galumphing back. Dan patted
him and gave him a bun.

"Now we must get you away from Bigshott," said Mr Oldcastle, "and find you a new home." He had no idea where: all he knew was that he'd never let the elephant return to that dreadful zoo. So they were off. Bunbo loped behind the car as Dan fed him with more buns.

Soon they saw a village ahead and stopped.

"Wait here with Horace," said Mr Oldcastle, "while we get you some proper food."

He drove to the shops with Dan and they soon returned with a bale of hay and a sack of buns. But Bunbo had disappeared! There was only Horace, jumping around.

Just then a police car stopped beside them.
"There's a dangerous elephant on the run,"
said the sergeant. "If you see it, keep well
away and inform us." All at once it began to
rain, and before Mr Oldcastle could tell him
about Bunbo, the sergeant drove away
with sirens blaring. Then the rain
stopped just as suddenly.

But where was Bunbo?
Horace knew, sure enough,
and led the way.

There was Bunbo, sitting in a pond and spraying water merrily around. Mr Oldcastle tried to coax him out, but it was no good. Then Dan honked the horn, calling "Dinner's ready," which worked.

Bunbo soon finished the hay and there were buns all round. Feeling better, they set out again. Bunbo felt frisky and ran ahead. "Come back," called Mr Oldcastle and stepped on the gas.

Bunbo ran so fast that he nearly collided with a farmer, who promptly leaped over the hedge and ran for dear life. Bunbo scooped up a barrowful of turnips and charged on.

Mr Oldcastle, trying to catch up, was dismayed to see Bunbo brush past a flower-lady's table and upset it. She nearly fainted at the sight of a charging elephant munching her flowers.

Gumdrop was way behind when suddenly the engine stopped. No petrol – and no Bunbo! So Mr Oldcastle honked the horn in its special way. An answering call came, sure enough, and Bunbo returned, still munching the flowers.

He was a naughty elephant, but clever. He lowered his head and pushed Gumdrop to a garage for petrol. Then he strolled across to a stall and helped himself to a bunch of bananas. The vegetable man had to watch his entire stock disappear by the trunkful.

As they continued their journey, Bunbo stopped by a stream for a drink but Gumdrop went on. All of a sudden a big truck blocked the road and a furious Barmy Bigshott leaped out brandishing his gun, which went off with a deafening roar.

"Gotcha at last!" he yelled. "Gimme back me elephant now, pronto, or else!"

"Most certainly not!" retorted Mr Oldcastle. "You'd only starve him again in that dreadful zoo of yours."

Just then Bunbo re-appeared and uncurled his trunk.

Then he spurted a jet of water at Bigshott that made
the man fall flat on his back. With another jet he soaked
all the plugs on the truck's engine.

"Well done, Bunbo," said Mr Oldcastle, impressed.
"But we'd better be off before he dries out."

So they hurried on, leaving Bigshott far behind. But
before long there was another hold-up.

A big red tractor barred the way. In it
sat the farmer, the flower-lady and the vegetable man.
"There's the elephant!" they shouted.
"He stole my turnips!"
"He ate my flowers!"
"He pinched all my vegetables!"
Mr Oldcastle gave a wad of money to Bunbo. "We're
very sorry, but I hope that this will cover your costs," he
said. Bunbo poked the money into the cab and the
tractor drove away in a cloud of dust.
"I hope we shan't be held up again," said Mr Oldcastle
– but he spoke too soon.

This time it was the police sergeant blocking the road ahead with his car, and from behind came the big truck and Barmy Bigshott with his gun!

"'ere's the thief, copper," he yelled. "Nick 'im!"
The sergeant, who now knew what had happened, told Mr Oldcastle to return the elephant to its legal owner. "Otherwise you are under arrest."

"Oh no he's not!" boomed a commanding voice, and everyone turned in astonishment.

It was Mr Oldcastle's good friend Sir Marmaduke Ricketty-Cobwebb, in his Rolls-Royce Silver Ghost.

"I'm the local magistrate and I have a warrant for the arrest of one Barmy Bigshott, for serious offences under the Protection of Animals Act. Officer, do your duty."

"With pleasure, Sir," said the sergeant, and he handcuffed Bigshott in a flash. "And while we are about it," he added, "you are also charged with possession of a dangerous weapon. Come quietly now."

"Now then," said Sir Marmaduke, "this elephant needs a home. Well, I have a new safari park at Mildew Manor – just the place for him." So he led the way in his Ghost, followed by Bunbo, Gumdrop and Horace in happy procession.

At the safari park Bunbo saw another elephant. Her name was Mambo and she trumpeted her welcome. Bunbo shook Mr Oldcastle's hand (with his trunk), and galumphed down to meet Mambo, trumpeting merrily. He sounded just like Gumdrop's horn.

Ever since that day, Gumdrop has been a regular visitor to Mildew Safari Park. The other animals from Barmy Bigshott's Zoo are there too, happy in their new home.

Happiest of all is Bunbo, with Mambo and their baby elephant. So when he visits, Dan has to bring an extra-large supply of buns to feed them all.

ISBN 1-84135-330-2

First published 1990 by Hodder and Stoughton Children's Books
This revised edition first published 2004 by Award Publications Limited,
27 Longford Street, London NW1 3DZ

Printed in Malaysia